D0385824

MORE TALES
OF
OLIVER PIG

Jean Van Leeuwen

PICTURES BY

ARNOLD LOBEL

Dial Books for Young Readers · NEW YORK

Dial easy-to-read

Published by
Dial Books for Young Readers
2 Park Avenue
New York, New York 10016

Published simultaneously in Canada
by Fitzhenry & Whiteside Limited, Toronto
Text copyright © 1981 by Jean Van Leeuwen
Pictures copyright © 1981 by Arnold Lobel
Printed in Hong Kong by South China Printing Co.
COBE
4 6 8 10 9 7 5 3

The Dial Easy-to-Read logo is a trademark of
Dial Books for Young Readers,
a division of NAL Penguin Inc., ® TM 1,162,718.

Library of Congress Cataloging in Publication Data
Van Leeuwen, Jean. More tales of Oliver Pig.
Summary: The further adventures of Oliver Pig and his family.
[1. Pigs—Fiction.] I. Lobel, Arnold. II. Title.
PZ7.V3273Mo [E] 80-23289
ISBN 0-8037-8713-8 (pbk.)
ISBN 0-8037-8714-6 (lib. bdg.)

The art for each picture consists of an ink
and wash drawing with two color overlays,
all reproduced as halftone.

Reading Level 1.9

For David,
my own little Oliver

CONTENTS

THE SURPRISE SEED

Father and Oliver

were making a garden.

First they raked the dirt.

Then they made

five very straight rows.

Then they dropped in the seeds

and covered them up.

The first row was radishes.

Next was string beans.

Then cucumbers.

Then squash.

And last was pumpkins.

"Now our garden is ready to grow,"
said Father.

Oliver saw something in the grass.

"Look, Father," he said. "A seed."

"We must have dropped one,"
said Father.

Father made a place

for Oliver's seed,

and Oliver dropped it in.

"What kind of seed is it?"

he asked.

"We will have to wait and see,"

said Father.

"It will be a surprise."

The next morning Oliver went to see

his surprise seed.

"Father," he said,

"there is nothing here."

"Not yet," said Father.

"We must wait awhile.

The sun will shine

and the rain will fall.

Soon a little plant will come up."

The sun shone and the rain fell.

One morning Oliver saw
something green poking up
where his seed was planted.
"Father, my plant came up,"
said Oliver.
"So it did," said Father.
"What kind of plant is it?"
asked Oliver.

"I think it is a squash plant,"
said Father.

"I like squash," said Oliver.
"When can I eat some?"

"Not yet," said Father.

"We must wait
for your plant to grow bigger."

Every day Father and Oliver worked
in the garden.
Oliver made shade for his plant
when the sun was too hot.
He watered it
when the rain did not fall.
Soon it had flowers.
And one day a baby squash.

"Now can I eat it?" asked Oliver.

"Not quite yet," said Father.

"We must wait for the squash

to grow bigger."

"This is a lot of waiting,"

said Oliver.

"It is a lot of growing,"

said Father.

Oliver's baby squash grew bigger.

And bigger.

And one day Father said,

"We will have your squash

for dinner tonight."

Oliver carried his squash

into the kitchen.

"Oh, my," said Mother.

"I will have to use

my biggest cooking pot."

At suppertime there was a platter

of meat on the table,

and a bowl of potatoes,

and a big bowl of Oliver's squash.

Mother took a bite.

"Delicious," she said.

Father took a bite.

"Delectable," he said.

Amanda took a bite.

"Ummy," she said.

"I grew it myself,"

said Oliver.

"I think that is what makes it

taste so good,"

said Father.

"More," said Amanda.

And they all had a lot more

of Oliver's squash.

ALL ALONE

"What are you doing?" asked Oliver.

"I am going to hang up the wash,"
said Mother.

"I will help you," said Oliver.

Oliver reached into the basket

and pulled out his sailor suit

and Amanda's dress

and Father's pajama bottoms.

"Oh, here is my baseball hat,"
he said.

He dropped the dress
and pajama bottoms in the mud.

"Oh, Oliver!" said Mother.

Amanda climbed
into the basket.

"Uh-oh," she said.

All the clothes fell

out in the mud.

"Oh, Amanda!" said Mother.

She took all the clothes inside

and put them back in the washer.

"What are you going to do now?"

asked Oliver.

"Clean the bedroom,"

said Mother.

"I will help you," said Oliver.

Mother got out the mop.

Oliver got out the broom.

Amanda got out the dustpan.

They started cleaning.

But the mop and the broom

and the dustpan got all tangled up.

Amanda fell down.

Oliver bumped his head.

Mother put away the mop.

"You are good helpers," she said.

"But some jobs are better for one

than for three."

Mother sat down

in the big chair.

"What are you doing now?"

asked Oliver.

"Resting," said Mother.

Amanda climbed into Mother's lap.

Oliver got his circus book.

"Read to me," he said.

"Not now," said Mother.

"Now I would like a quiet time.

I would like to be alone."

"Alone?" said Oliver.

"You wouldn't like it.

You would be lonesome."

"I don't think so," said Mother.

"Come outside."

Mother and Oliver and Amanda
went outside.

"Would you and Amanda like to make
a mud pie for dinner?" asked Mother.

"Yes," said Oliver.

"Good," said Mother.

"Put plenty of raisins in it.
I am going to be alone."

Mother climbed high
in the apple tree.
She sat in the seat
that Father had built
and did nothing all alone.

29

Oliver and Amanda made a mud pie
with plenty of raisins.

"We finished the pie," said Oliver.

"Are you lonesome?"

"No," said Mother.

"Why don't you make
some pudding now?"

Oliver and Amanda made a big dish
of chocolate pudding.

"Are you lonesome yet?"

asked Oliver.

"No," said Mother.

"How about a birthday cake?"

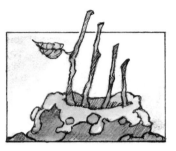

Oliver and Amanda made

a birthday cake

with strawberry icing

and four candles on top.

"That is a beautiful cake,"

said Mother.

"You came down!" said Oliver.

"Yes," said Mother.

"I got lonesome

for my Oliver and Amanda."

"I knew you would," said Oliver.

"You are covered with mud,"

said Mother.

"Let's go take a bubble bath."

"Together?" asked Oliver.

"Together," said Mother.

And they did.

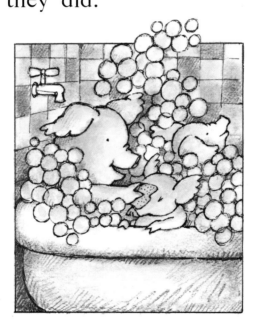

QUESTIONS

Father and Oliver

went walking

in the snow.

"Father," said Oliver,

"how many snowflakes are up

in the sky?"

"So many," said Father,

"that no one can count them all."

"I can count to one hundred,"
said Oliver.

"There are even more than that,"
said Father.

"Millions and millions."

Father and Oliver looked down
at the ground.

"Father," said Oliver,

"where did the garden go

when the snow came?"

"It is still there," said Father,

"sleeping under the snow

until spring comes."

"When spring comes,

will my flowers come back?"

asked Oliver.

"Not the same ones," said Father.

"But under the ground

the beginnings of new flowers

are waiting.

When the sun warms the earth,

they will come up."

Father and Oliver looked up

at the trees.

"Father," said Oliver,

"where do the birds go

when it snows?"

"Some fly away to warmer places,"
said Father.

"And some stay in their nests,
where it is snug and warm."

"Is our house like a nest?"
asked Oliver.

"Yes," said Father.

"And now I think it is time for us
to go inside and get snug and warm."

Father and Oliver took off

their snow clothes.

"Father," said Oliver,

"why are my toes still cold?"

"It takes a few minutes for the warm

to get to your toes," said Father.

"But I know what will help."

Father made two cups of hot cocoa.

Then he and Oliver sat

in the big chair next to the fire.

"Father," said Oliver,

"when you were little,

did your father know

just how to warm you up?"

"Yes," said Father.

"He always did."

Father took a book from the shelf.

"Here is a picture of my father
and me when I was little," he said.

"But why does that picture
look just like my father and me?"
asked Oliver.

"Because Grandfather and you and I
are all in the same family,"
said Father.

"Father," said Oliver,

"when you were little, where was I?"

"When I was little,
you had not yet been born,"
said Father.

"It is like the flowers

in our garden waiting for spring.

Everything has a time to grow.

And now, little Oliver,

I have a question for you."

"What is it?" asked Oliver.

"Why do you ask so many questions?"

asked Father.

"I think it is because I want
to know a lot of things,"
said Oliver.
Father hugged Oliver.
"Someday I think you will know
a lot of things," he said.
"Father," said Oliver,
"my toes are warm now."
"I am glad," said Father.

MOTHER'S HOLIDAY

"Have a nice day," said Mother.

"I will be home in time for supper."

Oliver and Amanda waved until

they couldn't see Mother anymore.

"What is Mother going to do?"

asked Oliver.

"She is having a holiday,"

said Grandmother.

"What is a holiday?" asked Oliver.

"It is a day when you do just what you want to do," said Grandmother.

"I would like to have a holiday," said Oliver.

"Someday you will," said Grandmother.

"Now let's have breakfast."

Grandmother put Oliver's egg on his plate.

"Something is wrong with my egg," said Oliver. "It's all juicy."

"It is a perfect sunny-side-up egg,"
said Grandmother.

"I don't want a sunny-side-up egg,"
said Oliver.

"Mother always makes scrambled eggs.
With cheese."

Grandmother cooked scrambled eggs
with cheese for Oliver and Amanda.
She ate the sunny-side-up egg
herself.

"What would you like to do today?"
asked Grandmother.

"I want to build a road in the dirt
for my cars," said Oliver.

"Shall I help you?"
asked Grandmother.

"No," said Oliver.

"Mother always stays inside.
You stay here and clean the house."

For lunch Grandmother made
peanut butter sandwiches.

"Too much peanut butter,"
said Oliver.

"Mother doesn't put in

so much peanut butter."

"The more peanut butter, the better,

I always say," said Grandmother.

Oliver took a bite.

"I'm all full," he said.

After lunch

Oliver got out his cars

and built a racetrack.

Then he got out his blocks

and built a city.

Then he and Amanda

knocked everything down.

"Let's paint pictures," said Oliver.

"First you must clean up
this big mess," said Grandmother.

"You help me," said Oliver.

"I can't," said Grandmother.

"My knees are too old."

"Mother always helps me,"
said Oliver. "I want Mother."

"Mama!" Amanda began to cry.

Grandmother held Amanda on her lap
in the rocking chair.

She sang her a soft song.

"More," said Amanda.

Grandmother sang a song about a sailing ship.

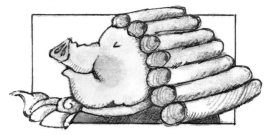

And a song about a pig's wig.

And a song about the smile on a crocodile.

"Mother never does this,"
said Oliver. "I like it."
"After you clean up,"
said Grandmother,
"we will sing some more."
When Mother came home,
they were still singing.
"Did you have a nice day?"
asked Mother.
"Yes," said Oliver.
"Grandmother made me
a perfect sunny-side-up egg
and a sandwich with a lot
of peanut butter.

I cleaned up a big mess myself
and we sang songs."
"That sounds very nice,"
said Mother.
"Grandmother," said Oliver,
"will you make me another
sunny-side-up egg tomorrow?"
"Not tomorrow," said Grandmother.
"Tomorrow I am having a holiday."

BEDTIME

"Mother," called Oliver.

"What is it?" asked Mother.

"I can't sleep," said Oliver.

"Why can't you sleep?" asked Mother.

"Maybe I am cold," said Oliver.

Mother pulled up Oliver's quilt.

"Good night, Oliver," she said.

Mother closed the door.

"Mother," called Oliver.

"What is it?" asked Mother.

"I can't sleep," said Oliver.

"Why can't you sleep?" asked Mother.

"Maybe I am thirsty," said Oliver.

"Bring me a drink of water."

"Please," said Mother.

"Please," said Oliver.

Mother gave Oliver a drink of water.

"Good night, Oliver," she said.

Mother closed the door.

"Mother," called Oliver.

"What is it?" asked Mother.

"I can't sleep," said Oliver.

"Why can't you sleep?" asked Mother.

"Maybe I am lonesome," said Oliver.

"I need some animals in my bed."

"You have your tiger," said Mother.

"I need a lot of animals,"
said Oliver.

Mother put Oliver's elephant
and his duck and his big bear
and his baby bear in his bed.

"Good night, Oliver," she said.

Mother closed the door.

"Mother," called Oliver.

"What is it?" asked Mother.

"I can't sleep," said Oliver.

"Why can't you sleep?" asked Mother.

"Maybe I am hot," said Oliver.

"And my ear itches

and I can't scratch it

because I am tucked in too tight."

"Your ear wouldn't itch

if you were asleep," said Mother.

Mother took off Oliver's quilt.

Oliver scratched his ear.

"Good night, Oliver," she said.

Mother closed the door.

"Mother," called Oliver.

"What is it?" asked Mother.

"I can't sleep," said Oliver.

"Why can't you sleep?" asked Mother.

"Maybe I am still lonesome,"
said Oliver.

"I think I need a big hug."

Mother gave Oliver a big hug.

"I think I need one too,"
said Mother.

Oliver gave Mother a big hug.

"Grrrrrrr," he said.

"What was that?" asked Mother.

"A bear hug," said Oliver.

Mother yawned.

"All this hugging

is making me sleepy," she said.

Oliver yawned.

"Me too," he said.

Mother tucked Oliver in again.

"Good night, Oliver," she said.

"Good night, Mother," said Oliver.

And he was asleep

before she closed the door.